A CELEBRATION OF GOD'S CREA

HIP ★ HIP ★ HIP

Hippopotamus

BY MARY RICE HOPKINS
ILLUSTRATED BY WENDY FRANCISCO

CROSSWAY BOOKS • WHEATON, ILLINOIS
A DIVISION OF GOOD NEWS PUBLISHERS

DEDICATION

From the Author:
To Trisha and David

From the Artist:
To Annie

Hip Hip Hip Hippopotamus

Copyright © 1996 by Mary Rice Hopkins

Published by Crossway Books, a division of Good News Publishers,
1300 Crescent Street, Wheaton, Illinois 60187

Art Director: Brian Ondracek

Cover Design: Jim Hilborn

First printing, 1996

Printed in Mexico

Library of Congress Cataloging-in-Publication Data
Hopkins, Mary Rice.
  Hip, hip, hip hippopotamus: a celebration of God's creation   /
written by Mary Rice Hopkins : illustrated by Wendy Francisco.
    p.   cm.
  Summary: Rhyming text presents a humorous celebration of God's
creation, from the sea and forest to the hippopotamus.
  ISBN 0-89107-905-X
  [1. Creation—Fiction.   2. Stories in rhyme.]   I. Francisco,
Wendy, ill.   II. Title.
PZ8.3.H7765H1   1996
[E]—dc20   96-25851

05	04	03	02	01	00	99	98	97
15	14	13	12	11	10	9	8	7	6	5	4	3

A MESSAGE TO PARENTS

Do you ever find yourself in awe of all that God has made? *Hip Hip Hip Hippopotamus* is a fun story-song that celebrates His wonderful creation and our uniqueness. Here's a great way to share with your children how special they are and that God even made something as fun as the hippo!

So take this opportunity to enjoy the wonderful illustrations by my good friend Wendy. Find the hidden hippos in the sea, the trees, and the sky and explain how God has arranged every detail in our lives too. Snuggle up close with your kids and always remember to look for God's fingerprints in His unique creation.

Mary Rice Hopkins

In the beginning

God made

the sea,

and the forest filled with trees.

He made the mountains

up so high,

On the very top He placed the sky.

God's fingerprints are everywhere,
just to show how much He cares.

In between He had loads of fun,

He made a hippo who weighs a ton.

Hip hip hip hippopotamus!
Hip hip hooray! God made all of us.

Hip hip hip hippopotamus!
Hip hip hooray! He made us.

Creation sings of His praise,

the sparrow

and the tiny babe.

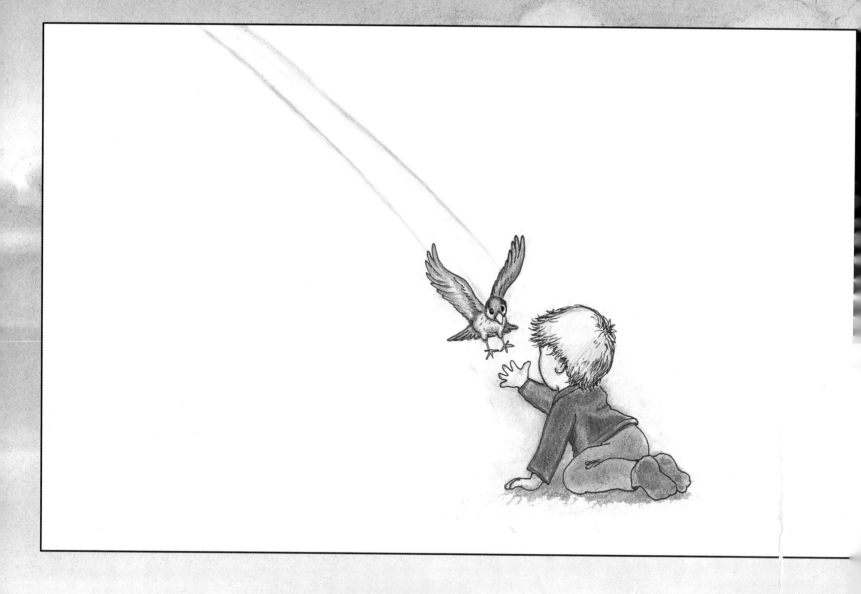

We can sing and say, "Well done."

But some things

He just made for fun.

Hip hip hip hippopotamus!

Hip hip hooray! He made us.

The End.